DATE DUE			

Schaumburg Township District Library
KIDSZONE
Central Branch
130 South Roselle Road
Schaumburg, Illinois 60193

For Seraphina, of course

Library of Congress
Cataloging-in-Publication Data

Jordan, Mary Ellen.
Lazy Daisy, cranky Frankie /
by Mary Ellen Jordan & Andrew Weldon.
p. cm.
Summary: During the day on an unusual farm, Daisy the lazy cow would rather eat
jelly than grass, Frankie the cranky dog watches television instead of sheep, and the other animals
behave equally oddly but at night, all are good at sleeping.
ISBN 978-0-8075-4400-6
[1. Stories in rhyme. 2. Domestic animals—Fiction. 3. Farms—Fiction. 4. Humorous stories.]
I. Weldon, Andrew, ill. II. Title.
PZ8.3.J7654Laz 2013
[E]—dc23
2012013281

Text copyright © 2011 by Mary Ellen Jordan and Andrew Weldon.
Illustrations copyright © 2011 by Andrew Weldon.
Published in 2013 by Albert Whitman & Company.
ISBN 978-0-8075-4400-6
First published in 2011 in Australia by Allen & Unwin.
Printed in the USA.
10 9 8 7 6 5 4 3 LB 18 17 16 15 14 13

The design is by Andrew Weldon and Bruno Herfst.

For more information about Albert Whitman & Company,
visit our web site at www.albertwhitman.com.

LAZY DAISY, CRANKY FRANKIE

Mary Ellen Jordan & Andrew Weldon

Albert Whitman & Company
Chicago, Illinois

This is my cow,
she's called Daisy.
She should eat grass,
but she's too lazy.

Instead she eats jelly,
spoon after spoon,

all through the morning
till late afternoon.

This is my pig,
she's called Nancy.

She should like mud, but she's too fancy.

Instead she stares
at her reflection,

"My oh my,
you are perfection."

This is my chicken,
she's called Lizzie.

She should lay eggs,
but she's too busy.

Instead she dances
through the air,

in her purple
underwear.

This is my dog, he's called Frankie.

He should chase sheep,
but he's too cranky.

Instead he slumps,
watching TV,

demanding cake
and cups of tea.

None of the animals
do what they should.

Except for at night . . .
there's no mooing or barking
or oinking or cheeping.

At least my animals
are good at sleeping.